A Secret
Shared

A Secret Shared

a novel by

Patricia MacLachlan

 KATHERINE TEGEN BOOKS

An Imprint of HarperCollins Publishers

Katherine Tegen Books is an imprint of HarperCollins Publishers.

A Secret Shared
Copyright © 2021 by Patricia MacLachlan
All rights reserved. Printed in the United States of America.

ISBN 978-0-06-288585-2

Typography by Molly Fehr
21 22 23 24 25 PC/LSCH 10 9 8 7 6 5 4 3 2 1
❖
First Edition

Children know many secrets—
Some they keep—
Some they find ways to bring into the light.

For Jamie and Lauren, Harry and Lucy.
Love, P. M.

1.

The Searcher

I watch my mother spit into a plastic tube. A pot of fresh flowers sits on her desk. Every week she walks to the cemetery to put flowers on the grave of her best friend from childhood.

"Flowers and spit?!" I say to her with a grin. "Funny combination! Why the tube?"

She smiles and hands me a pamphlet. "It's a new simple DNA service, Nora. For exploring your life. You can find out your ancestors. Where you came from."

She replaces the combs tightly holding back her long hair. She calls it her "professional" look.

"I'll write about it in my newspaper column," she says. "I'm always looking for new topics and replies."

I read the pamphlet direction words out loud.

WHO ARE YOU?
Where were your ancestors born?
Discover your past!

SPIT, PAY, MAIL your DNA.

At the kitchen table my father smiles.

My twin brother, Ben, raises his eyebrows.

My younger sister, Birdy, watches Mother spit, then goes back to turning the pages of her book. Birdy is becoming a reader.

"We learned about DNA in class," says Ben. "Your DNA is who you are. You send your spit sample and find out your nationality. And the family you came from."

"And maybe surprises," says Mother. "Sweet things in my past."

"What kind of sweet surprises, Mom?"

asks Ben. "More than you're Una Buckley from Ireland," he adds.

Sometimes Ben is "outspoken."

In class we had to write a sentence showing we knew the meaning of "outspoken." My sentence was "My brother Ben is outspoken."

It made my teacher laugh out loud.

I loved my third-grade teacher, Miss Schyler. We all call her Miss Skylark. I still love her. I talk to her every day after school when I need to—and when I wait for Birdy and Ben to walk home. Miss Skylark always listens.

"My friend Ellie's mother found ancestors in three different countries," I say.

"Our principal found a new cousin he dislikes," says Ben, making Mother and Father laugh.

"Whatever it is, I'll find out!" says Mother.

"'The searcher,' your mother," says Father.

Mother writes a column for the town newspaper on topics that interest her. She used to work at the newspaper office in town but likes working at home best.

She has a kitchen alcove with her desk and computer.

She put her nameplate in front of the computer—with her Irish name and her married name—

Una Buckley Rossi

"It reminds you who I am," she told us, joking. "And that I'm working."

One new column is about bullies.

Una's View

Do you know a bully?

Are *you* a bully?

Have you been bullied?

Tell me.

—Una Rossi

The column received over two dozen answers to this question. Mother's favorite response was from Robert.

I was young when I was bullied. I got help.

Now I'm a therapist and help others.

—Robert M.

Her column on goats brought responses
from two family members.

Una's View

GOATS!

Try goats to clear out your messy yards and

woods instead of loud lawnmowers and

chain saws. One local service brings an

expandable fence, and three goats who will

eat everything, even poison ivy!

—Una Rossi

Goats?! Are you kidding me?!

—Jill

Great idea! I hate mowing.

—Jill's husband

"I used to write poetry," Mother tells us. "But when I write a poem it flies up and away into the air. I guess I like quick responses—voices coming back to me."

"The searcher," repeats Father, kissing Mother on the top of her head. "I have to work now."

Our father is a university art professor and sculptor of clay, stone, and recently wood.

Mother holds out the DNA padded envelope for him.

"I wrote permission for another DNA searcher. All you have to do is sign," says Mother.

Father shakes his head. He will not spit in a tube.

"I know where I came from," he says. "And I know where I'm going."

"Where did you come from, Papa?" asks Birdy, looking up from her book.

"I'm Giovanni Rossi!" he says. "'Geo' to your mama. From Italy!"

"And where are you going?" asks Ben with a smile.

"To buy a new special sculpting saw," he

says. "Do you know when winter comes I can actually sculpt ice?"

"But it will just melt," says Mother.

Father sighs.

"Yes. That's part of the beauty of it, Una," he says. "It's there and then changes as it melts."

Surprising us, Mother goes over to him, stands on her tiptoes, and kisses him.

"Kissing!" says Birdy.

"I don't get you," Mother says to him.

"I don't always get you either," he says. "But it's all right. You may think that you'll find 'sweet' things in the past, Una. But they're here. In the present."

"Like us," says Ben stubbornly.

"And me!" adds Birdy.

Father goes out the door with a wave to us.

Birdy, named Beatrix but called Birdy by us, closes her book and stands up.

"I want to spit!" she announces.

"Of course you want to spit in a tube!" says Ben.

He hands her a tube. "Here, Birdy."

Birdy spits and misses. She spits again.

Mother looks up suddenly.

"Don't put Birdy's spit sample in the return envelope," she says.

We hear her careful strong tone.

"Okay," says Ben.

Mother's phone rings.

I put the open envelope on the table.

"Let's read in Nora's room," says Ben.

"Come, Birdy," I say.

"Coming!" calls Birdy as we walk down the hall. "I'm getting more books."

We should have known—looking back later—that Birdy is beginning a new story.

2.
Truth

Weeks go by. Birdy reads all the time now. She has her very own library card. She reads to my captive father for so long at night he sometimes falls asleep.

"I hear her sweet voice in my dreams," he says.

Mother still searches—for topics for her

column, for things unknown—maybe for "sweet" things in her past?

I read her column from yesterday.

Una's View

Do you know your ancestors?

How important is family, past and present?

What is the most important thing you owe your family?

I'm looking for truth.

Tell me.

—Una Rossi

The truth? I've never seen her ask for the "truth" in her column before. Just responses.

What truth is she looking for?

One response the next day is simple:

I owe my family everyday truths.

That's *my* truth that you asked for.

—Bella

Father's students visit his studio in the side yard, swarming around his sculptures, his stone pieces, his sculpting tools and wood supply.

The students love his new specially made sculpting saw. He has a tall piece of a tree leaning outside against his studio.

"How did that get here?!" I ask.

"I dragged it myself," Father says

proudly. "Maybe *I'm* 'the *true* searcher.'"

Ben shakes his head.

"It's only a dead tree, Dad," he says.

"My idea of a treasure," says Father. "You'll see one day."

Ben and I walk to school every day, Birdy sometimes reading to us as one of us holds on to her. Sometimes she skips ahead. We pass the bakery and the library.

Today Mother walks partway with us, carrying a pot of white lilies for her best friend's grave.

We stop as she opens the cemetery gate and goes in, waving goodbye to us. We never go in—it's Mother's private time. There's nothing there for us.

We walk on to school.

Birdy's a favorite of the morning crossing guard, Billy.

"Good day, Miss Birdy," he says.

"It's going to rain, Billy," says Birdy.

"Not on me," says Billy. "I'll be home."

"With Mrs. Billy," says Birdy, making Billy grin.

"I'm going to start calling my wife Mrs. Billy now," Billy says. "Better yet, her first name is Millie!"

We all laugh.

"Is that the truth?" asks Birdy.

"The truth," says Billy.

That word again.

We watch Birdy skip all the way to school, chanting, "Millie Billy—Millie Billy—Millie Billy!"

My favorite teacher, Miss Skylark, isn't in her room after school. Ben, Birdy, and I find her outside on bus duty. Birdy was right. It's beginning to rain.

"I can read!" Birdy tells Miss Skylark.

"Yay. Best news of the day!" says Miss Skylark. "All those books! Soon you will be a writer, Birdy. Books can show you the way! They did that for Nora. And Ben, too. Nora writes wonderful essays. Ben's words are strong as a 'speaker.'"

Ben grins at her.

"You think so?" asks Birdy.

Miss Skylark nods. She takes a plastic bag out of her pocket.

"Here, Birdy. Keep your books dry."

Birdy hugs Miss Skylark. We hurry on.

Aggie, the afternoon crossing guard, holds a large umbrella over us as we cross the street.

"Thank you, Aggie!" we call as Ben and I take Birdy's hands and run in the rain.

When we get home and open the front door—shaking raindrops off us—Birdy takes her dry books to her room.

Ben and I see Mother opening a large envelope.

The DNA envelope.

The news she has waited for—whatever it will be—the truth.

3.

Birdy

Mother reads her DNA report silently. Then she looks at us.

"No royalty in this report," she says. "No drama. No magic. I'll have to search further for 'sweet surprises.'"

"Are you disappointed?" I ask.

Mother holds up a finger and thumb, showing an inch.

"A little," she says.

"But you *are* Irish?" asks Ben.

"That I am," says Mother.

She tosses the envelope to Ben as her phone rings. She answers, her back to us.

A paper falls out of the envelope, and Ben picks it up. He stares at it. He looks quickly at my mother, but she's still on the phone.

He hands the paper to me. His face is suddenly pale.

Mother doesn't turn around to see it.

I read the paper and my hand shakes a

bit. I hide the paper in my pocket and take Ben's hand.

We hurry down the hallway.

In my bedroom I stare at Ben.

"Birdy put her spit in the envelope!" I whisper. "She wrote her name in the permission space."

Ben nods and closes the door.

"When no one was looking," he says.

"Birdy is Swedish," I say. "Not Irish or Italian."

I look at the word "Swedish."

"Birdy's ancestors were from Sweden?" I say.

Ben sits on my bed.

"Our parents are Irish and Italian. Not a match," he says softly.

His face is so sad that I sit close to him. He looks at me.

"Who is Birdy?" he asks.

I feel sudden anger. "We *know* who Birdy is!" I say fiercely.

Then softer—"We just don't know where she came from."

"Or who her parents were?" says Ben.

Tears fill his eyes. I've never ever seen Ben cry before. Never.

I know something about Ben that he doesn't know I know. He loves Birdy most of all the family. He has always watched over her, laughing at whatever she does, protecting her when she needs it.

I put an arm around Ben. "Birdy was adopted," I say. "By us."

Ben turns to look at me.

"But why the secret?" he says, his voice as fierce as mine had been. "Why?"

I shake my head.

"My friend Ellie was adopted, and she celebrates that day and her birthday," I say.

"And Birdy's friend Nico is adopted—and his little sister," says Ben.

Then Ben gets up and looks out the window. He turns around suddenly.

"What if it's a mistake, Nora?" he says. "The test could be wrong. We can try again."

"How?"

"Mother has another envelope. I saw it in her desk drawer. We could send another DNA test," he says. "I know where she keeps her credit card."

I am quiet.

"Should we do that?" I say softly.

"We have to," Ben says. "We can't forget what we already saw."

"Couldn't we just ask Mother and Father?"

Ben sighs. "Not until we know the truth."

I get up and look out the window with Ben.

"You know the truth can be scary," I say, watching the rain.

Ben nods. "Yes."

We stand together, watching the rain grow stronger.

This story is not mine anymore.

This story belongs to Birdy.

Ben has gone to bed.

But I don't sleep. I sit up thinking about Birdy. Worrying about her.

I stare out my window until night comes and it's too dark to see the trees or the falling rain.

In the night, when I fall asleep, I have dreams—dreams of someone knocking on the door—come to take Birdy away.

I sit up in bed, frightened, and hurry into Birdy's bedroom.

She is curled up with her stuffed horse, sleeping peacefully. Her light hair looks like gold in the nightlight. I think of Ben's dark hair, and mine.

I sit in my bedroom and wait for morning light. I think about Miss Skylark.

The rain ends.

I know what to do.

4.

One Question

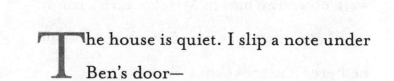

The house is quiet. I slip a note under Ben's door—

I've gone to school early.
Take care of Birdy.
—Nora.

I open the door quietly. I walk down the street—past the bakery and library—past the cemetery.

A woman working just inside the cemetery gate looks up and smiles at me.

I walk to the school. There are no school buses yet. Too early.

I open the big door and go inside, then walk down the hall to Miss Skylark's room.

She is sitting at her desk. I knew she'd be here. She looks up.

"Nora?"

She looks up at the clock. Then she beckons to me. "Come over here."

She pushes a chair close to her.

And I burst into tears and tell her

everything—the spit in the envelope, my mother's warning about Birdy's spit, what Birdy did—and about Birdy being Swedish.

I even tell her about my night dream that someone came to take Birdy away.

Miss Skylark listens to it all. She is quiet. She lets me cry.

There's a rustle at the door. Miss Skylark looks up. Ben stands there.

"I thought you'd be here," he says.

"Birdy?" I ask.

"Happy in the library," he says.

"Come in, Ben," says Miss Skylark.

He comes over to sit by me. He's still wearing his black sleep shirt with the many Zs on it.

Miss Skylark leans closer to us, her hands under her chin. She looks at Ben, then me.

"You two have a big secret," she says. "And you already know that a secret is hard to keep for now—just the two of you."

She pauses.

"I can think of one question to ask you right now," Miss Skylark says. "One question."

"What is that?" asks Ben.

Miss Skylark looks closely at the two of us.

"The question is this: Does it matter?"

We are quiet.

Does it matter?

"Until the problem is solved," Miss Skylark adds, "does it matter? Birdy is the sister you love. Does it matter where she came from? How she's come to be here?"

Miss Skylark is quiet then.

Suddenly the school bell rings. We can hear voices in the hallway.

The one question is like something new—a presence that follows us. It follows us after we say goodbye to Miss Skylark, through the day of classes, and at lunchtime.

It follows us when Ben and I walk home after school, Birdy skipping home with us.

"We learned about toads today," she says. "We visited the Kinder Garden. There is a pet toad there."

Ben and I smile at Birdy's name for "kindergarten."

"I'm going to look for the toad in our yard tonight. Sometimes they come back to the same home.

"You can help look," says Birdy.

Ben lifts his shoulders as if tossing something away.

"I'll help," he says.

"I'll help, too," I say.

"Can I use our flashlight at night?" Birdy asks Ben as she walks backward.

"Yes," says Ben. "Watch out for the curb, Birdy."

"Birdy!" says Aggie, stopping cars so we can cross.

"Aggie!" says Birdy, holding up her hand to touch Aggie's hand.

We walk past the cemetery. Past the library and the bakery.

"Miss Skylark was right," Ben says quietly.

I look sideways at him.

"It doesn't matter," he says, his voice calm and clear like Miss Skylark's voice.

I nod. I can't find words to say.

Ben holds his hand out and we link

fingers the way we did years ago when we were very little.

We have a pact, Ben and I.

Miss Skylark is right—

It doesn't matter.

5.

Secrets and Toads

It's night. Birdy holds the flashlight. Ben and I help hunt for the toad and his home.

Mother opens the back door, turning on the porch light.

"What are you doing out there?" she calls.

"Toad hunting!" calls Birdy. "Come help!"

Mother doesn't answer at first. She watches the flashlight in the darkness. I see her smile in the porch light.

"Happy hunting!" she calls, then closes the door.

Suddenly Birdy shouts. She is on her stomach, the flashlight shining on a stump at the edge of the woods.

"Look! I made a moss walkway to the hole in this stump," says Birdy. "And I put a bowl for water outside."

"You did all that?!" asks Ben.

"Last year when I was just a kid," says Birdy.

She looks up at us.

"See inside?"

Ben and I kneel down in the damp grass.

I catch my breath.

The flashlight shines on the red eyes of a toad, peering out. We can see his leaf green and brown body.

"My toad!" says Birdy, sounding like she might cry with happiness.

"My toad," she says more softly.

I feel like I might cry, too, at the joy of Birdy's voice.

Ben lies down in the grass next to Birdy. I lie down beside them. And we stay there until we shiver in the cool, damp grass.

The toad tires of us and backs into his safe, warm stump home.

Birdy comes into my bedroom after her shower. Her damp, light hair curls around her neck.

"Birdy, I have another tube for you to spit in."

"I get to spit again?!" asks Birdy, excited.

"Yep," says Ben.

He looks sideways at me.

"It's a secret, Birdy," he says carefully.

Another secret.

"Where's the tube?" asks Birdy. "I like spitting." Ben hands her the tube. She spits.

"I won't tell the secret," she says.

She thinks for a moment.

"Who do I not tell?" she asks very seriously.

Ben sighs. "It's all right, Birdy. The secret is for the three of us."

"Okay!" says Birdy.

She turns at the door.

"I love you two," she says quickly. Then she is out the door on her way down the hall to bed.

"We love you, too!" calls Ben after her.

Then it's quiet again. I know Ben is thinking of Birdy. Thinking of sending off a new secret search.

"You're feeling guilty," I say.

Ben shakes his head. "Sad," he says.

"I'm trying to remember Miss Skylark's words," I say.

He looks at me.

"And this may all be a mistake in the end, you know," he adds.

He starts to go out the door.

"Ben?"

He turns. "What?"

"Whatever happens—" I begin.

"Does it matter?" says Ben, finishing my sentence.

6.

Love

It's a two-day school break for teacher meetings.

"So the teachers can talk about us," Birdy tells us.

"I'm sure they talk about you all the time," says Father.

We all mill around the kitchen, my mother at her alcove desk.

"What's in Una's View today?" I ask.

Father hands me the newspaper, open to Una's View.

"It will interest you," he says.

I look at the column quickly, then at my father.

"It's about love!" I say, surprised.

"It is," he says.

I read.

Una's View

Let's Talk about Love!

My story—

Love painted me

before I knew love

It painted me

on a summer day

in a field of wild blooms.

I didn't see the painter

painting a copse of trees

high above me—

but he turned and painted me

alone—

not yet knowing love.

The painting is beautiful.

And because of the painter

I am now beautiful, too.

—Una Rossi

I stare at Mother. She's written a poem!

Not a regular column.

"I wanted a new topic," she says.

"But is this true?!" I ask.

"Yes," says my father, leaning against the kitchen counter. "I was the painter."

He sees my surprised look.

"I was a painter once," he says softly.

"It's a poem you wrote!" I say.

Mother shakes her head. She pulls her hair back tightly with combs.

"I don't write poetry anymore, remember? It's more of a scrambled essay," she says.

Father shakes his head, more to himself than to Mother.

"Where's the painting?" asks Birdy suddenly. "Why isn't it hanging up?"

"Good question, Birdy," says Ben.

"I think your mother is shy about some things—like hanging her portrait on our house walls," says Father.

Ben smiles a bit.

"But, Mom," he says, "you *did* write a very personal poem—or essay—about falling in love."

Father sits down at the kitchen table and looks over at Mother.

"Ben's right, Una," he says.

"Where is the painting?" Birdy repeats. "Mother wrote that it's beautiful."

"I don't think . . ." Mother begins. She looks over at Father.

"Oh, all right, Geo," she says, giving up.

Father gets up and goes to their bed-room. He comes back carrying a frame. He turns it around for us to see.

"Oh! That *is* beautiful!" I say.

The painting is Mother alone in a field filled with wild blooms, her hair around her shoulders.

"We were married in that field, your mother and I," says Father, remembering. "With a friend of mine, and Mother's best friend, Linnea."

"Linnea," says Birdy. "A beautiful name. Like the beautiful painting."

Father and Mother quickly look at each other, then away again.

"Did someone take pictures of your wedding?" asks Birdy.

"Maybe stashed somewhere—Geo and I will look for them one day," says Mother.

"I want the painting in my room!" says Birdy, excited. "Can we hang it on my wall?"

She looks at Mother.

"You won't be shy about it hanging in *my* room, will you?" asks Birdy.

Mother gets up and puts her arms around Birdy.

"No. I won't be shy. And every time I come to say goodnight I can see how beautiful the painting is."

"And you can see how I painted you into my life," says Father softly.

He picks Mother up, gently turning her around and around and around in his arms. She slips down, her hair combs falling to the floor, her hair around her shoulders like in the painting.

"Are they dancing?" Birdy whispers.

"Sort of," I say.

"There's no music," whispers Birdy.

"They don't seem to need music," Ben whispers back.

"They're loving each other," says Birdy, smiling.

And they dance around and around again.

I beckon to Birdy and Ben and we walk down the hall to our rooms—leaving Mother and Father alone—leaving Mother and Father "loving each other," in Birdy's words.

7.

Tillie

It's morning. I knock on Birdy's door.

"What?" she calls.

"Mother's making pancakes," I say.

I turn the doorknob. It's locked. I wait until Birdy unlocks the door and slides out, quickly shutting the door again.

"Are you up to something?" I ask.

"Maybe," says Birdy.

This makes me smile.

In the kitchen, Mother is happy, flipping pancakes and dancing to the table! She reminds me of Birdy skipping to school.

"What happened here?" I ask.

"Love did it," says Ben. "Her column had a 'high tide' of responses."

He has a plate of pancakes.

"Look at my computer, Nora!" says Mother. "'Let's Talk about Love'!"

She puts a tall stack of pancakes on the table with a flourish. She goes back to the stove.

"Thanks, Una. I think we have plenty," says Father.

Across the table Ben stretches up to look over the stack.

"You think?" he says, grinning.

I read Mother's responses.

> Yesterday an artist painted me on my horse and I fell off.
>
> He kissed me.
>
> I plan to fall off my horse again today.
>
> And tomorrow.
>
> It's Love.
>
> —Ella

My wife chased me when we were children.

It seemed fruitless to keep running.

—Married forever.

—Bud

I met my husband in the backseat of the
car driving us to preschool. We held hands
between our car seats. We have never
stopped.

—Rose

I found my dog Lulu in a field, just like
yours!

It is hard to paint how much I love her.

—Jess

A wonderful poem that tells us much about

love. And much about you. Thank you!

—Sheldon

I tried *not* to love my baby sister.

But I can't help it.

—Timmy

I'm a painter.

Where's the field?!

—Joe Z.

"I know Joe Z.," says Father. "Joe's one
of my painting students."

Mother laughs. "You made that up,
Geo."

"Nope. My painting student Joe Z. is looking for love."

I scroll down on dozens of responses.

"There are many responses about love," I tell Mother.

"*All* kinds of love," says Father. "One of my students loves his pet rabbit so much he brought it to college with him."

"Falling off a horse for love!" says Ben.

"And a loved dog found in a field of blooms," I say.

"Have you kissed again today?" asks Birdy, making Father smile.

"I will hug today," he says.

He gets up.

"I'm going off to plague my art

students," he says. "It's the day they show their photographs. I have a quote for them to think about."

"What's the quote?" asks Ben.

"The quote is from the photographer Diane Arbus. About photographs."

He puts it next to Ben's plate to read.

"A picture is a secret about a secret, the more it tells you, the less you know," Ben reads out loud.

I look up at Father.

"I don't know what that means," I say.

"Neither will my students," he says. "But it will make them think."

"I have a secret myself!!" blurts Birdy suddenly.

Ben's fork clatters to his plate, a startled look on his face. I think about the secret spit Ben sent to be tested.

"Want to tell us?" asks Mother.

"I'll show you!!"

Birdy runs to her room. She comes back with a kitten in her arms. I know what Birdy was hiding behind her door. The kitten is gray with white paws and face.

"My secret," Birdy says. "Can I keep her? I've already named her."

Birdy looks at Mother and Father.

"You're not mad, are you? Mad that I have a secret? You've had a secret, I bet. Lots of people have secrets, my teacher says."

Father looks at Mother. She is smiling.

"What's her name?" asks Father. He takes the kitten in his arms and holds her under his chin.

"Tillie," Birdy says happily, knowing that Tillie is hers to keep. "My friend Milo—across the street? The one who plays kick the can with me—his mother said to make sure to check with you before I keep her."

Tillie puts a tiny white paw up to my father's cheek.

"Tillie girl," he whispers, and he hands her to Mother. Mother holds her cuddled in her arms.

"I once had a gray cat named Mitzi," she says.

She hands Tillie to me. Tillie yawns and curls up in my lap, her body warm.

"Now, I have two very important things to say, and then I'm leaving for class," says Father.

"What?" asks Birdy.

"First, buy a litter box for Tillie soon," he says. "The second important thing is that I will now hug you all goodbye."

And he does—Birdy and Ben and me.

And when he hugs Mother he slips a sparkling jeweled comb out of her hair and we see him put it in his pocket.

Birdy puts her hand over her mouth and points.

Mother's hair tumbles to her shoulders. She is becoming the woman in his painting.

8.

Beautiful Sense

It's Saturday morning. We are surprised to find Father painting on the sun porch—a canvas of colors over colors.

"You're not in your studio," I say.

"I like the morning light here," he says, still painting in light strokes.

"Where's your dead tree?" asks Ben, looking out the window.

"I've been working on it inside. Out of the rain. I'll bring it out later to surprise you."

"What is that?" asks Birdy, pointing to his painting.

"I don't know yet," says Father.

"Aren't you supposed to know?" asks Birdy.

Father nods. "I'll know when I'm finished."

"Like finishing a book," says Birdy.

Father smiles and paints.

"And like my poetry," says Mother. "I

never know what I'm really saying until I get to the end."

"That makes beautiful sense," says Ben.

Father looks quickly at Ben.

"Do you mind that we're talking while you paint?" Birdy asks.

"Not now," he says. "I'm almost done."

He steps back, holding his brush. He paints again.

"There," he says to himself.

And when we look up at the painting of color there is a bird flying out of the painting into a sky we can't see.

"Miss Skylark once said it's heroic to make something beautiful out of a blank page," I say. "With art or words."

"Beautiful sense," says Ben as if he likes saying it.

Father steps back to look at his painting. He smiles.

"I'm liking painting again," he says, looking surprised. "That bird just flew in and out of my painting."

"Like the words in a poem," says Mother thoughtfully.

"Maybe I'll like writing poetry again, too."

"Beautiful sense, Una," says Father.

We leave Father with his painting and walk to the vegetable market. I pull the shopping cart behind me for Tillie's litter box and litter. Mother carries an armful of flowers, yellow and white.

"A cemetery worker gave me a vase left behind—he'll water the flowers for me," says Mother.

"That's nice," I say.

"He's been there a long time," says Mother.

"You too," says Ben.

"What's her name?" asks Birdy. "Your friend."

Mother doesn't answer but opens the gate.

"You want to walk ahead to the market? Or wait for me?" she asks.

"Wait," says Birdy.

And Mother goes inside.

I take out a small notebook to write a list.

"What do we want to buy at the market?" I ask.

"Vegetables!" Birdy and Ben say at the same time.

"Of course," Ben says to Birdy. "That's all you eat!"

They make up a verse together.

Tomatoes
Carrots
Squash and dill.
Corn and lettuce,
Eat your fill!!

After a while Mother comes out of the cemetery, waving to the caretaker.

We all walk away to the market, Birdy skipping all the way, singing the verse—

> Tomatoes
> Carrots
> Squash and dill.
> Corn and lettuce,
> Eat your fill!!

"Where did *that* come from?" asks Mother.

"Birdy and Ben made it up," I say. "They're kind of a pair, don't you think?"

Mother nods.

"I'd say you and Ben are a pair, too. He knows what you're thinking most times."

"And I know everything he thinks," I say.

"In the way of twins," says Mother.

"I like that—'in the way of twins,'" I say.

"Twins know each other. When you were toddlers you and Ben knew things about each other that Geo and I didn't know," says Mother.

Ben comes over and takes the shopping cart from me.

"I know you're tired of pulling this along," he says. "I'll take over."

Mother smiles at me.

"Twins," she says.

People smile at Ben and Birdy as they pick out vegetables. And when they dance

home while I pull the litter box in the gro-
cery cart.

"Ben is not embarrassed to look silly,"
I say.

Mother looks sideways at me and says
something I don't expect.

"It's Ben's 'beautiful sense,'" she says.

I am quiet for a moment.

"Do I have a beautiful sense, too?" I ask
Mother.

She nods and takes my hand.

"You have kindness," she says.

And we walk, holding hands, watching
Ben and Birdy laugh and chant all the way
home, Ben pulling the shopping cart.

But when we open our backyard gate all

noise suddenly stops.

"The dead tree," says Ben softly.

Father's tall tree stands—bark stripped away.

It is smoothed into a figure looking away—hair falling like water—catching something small. *The sparkling hair comb.*

Birdy points at the sparkling comb.

"Mama," she says.

"Yes."

Mother and I still hold hands. She smiles.

She knows herself in wood.

"Beautiful sense," she whispers.

9.

"Eyes and Art"

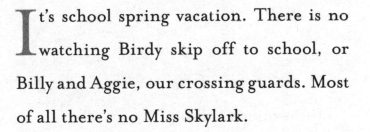

It's school spring vacation. There is no watching Birdy skip off to school, or Billy and Aggie, our crossing guards. Most of all there's no Miss Skylark.

Father is at the table with a cup of coffee.

Mother's not at her alcove desk.

"Where is Mom?" Ben asks.

"She left a note on her desk," Father
says.

Gone to an all-day poetry writing class.

To make beautiful sense.

Mother

Mom

Mama

"Is this true?" I ask.

Father nods. "True."

"Mom can be surprising, can't she,"
says Ben, making Father laugh a lot.

Birdy points to the "Mother, Mom, Mama."

"She signed the note with all the names we call her. Did you see?"

Then she points to the words "beautiful sense."

"What do these words mean?" Birdy asks.

"It means your mama is being very brave," Father tells her.

"She's going to learn more about poetry," I tell Birdy.

"Like going to school?" asks Birdy.

Ben nods.

"That *is* brave!" says Birdy.

Father taps Birdy's shoulder. He picks up his painting of Mother.

"Time to hang this," he says.

The four of us go into Birdy's bedroom.

Tillie sits in the window, watching birds, making small chattering sounds.

Father smiles at Birdy's cardboard litter box, with her hand-painted figures on the sides—a bird perched on a limb and the tail of a mouse disappearing into tall grass. Inside the box are strips of paper scattered around.

"A work of art, that box," he tells Birdy.

"Birdy made it when Tillie was a secret," I say.

"I cut up the newspaper into strips. Not Mother's column," she adds. "Tillie likes to scramble around in it before she sleeps with Charles and me."

"Who's Charles?" Father asks.

Birdy holds up her stuffed horse.

"My horse. It's named after my best friend Charles at school. We climb very high on the jungle gym and do tricks until the teachers run to tell us to get down."

Father grins.

"I put the new litter box in the back hallway," he says. "We'll show it to Tillie after I hang the painting."

He wipes the frame of the painting with

a cloth. He picks up his hammer and a picture hook.

"Where?" he asks Birdy.

Birdy points to the wall across from her bed.

"There," she says. "I can lie in bed and look at it."

Father nods.

He hammers in the picture hook. He hangs the painting—steps back, then adjusts it a bit.

"There," he says.

"Come lie down and look," says Birdy, excited.

Father lies down. Ben lies down. I squeeze into the space left.

"See how it looks from here?" says Birdy.

"It's a good painting," Father says softly. "I like seeing it on this wall."

"It's beautiful there," says Ben.

"It's beautiful anywhere," I say.

"I see Mother young," says Birdy.

"Eyes and art," says Father quietly.

I look over at him.

"What does that mean?"

"We see art with different eyes. You see Mother young. I see the woman I loved even as I painted her."

"Even then?" I ask.

"Even then," he says.

Eyes and art.

There are no words then.

Tillie jumps up on the bed, finding a space by Father. Birdy gathers her horse Charles into her arms.

There are no words.

10.

Unlocked

We move from the quiet of Birdy's bedroom to the noise of the back hallway.

There are lots of words.

Tillie's new litter box sits, unfilled yet, next to my parents' hall cupboard.

In school we've been learning how plays are written—mostly "dialogue" as Miss Skylark says. And "action."

"Tillie likes a painted litter box," says Birdy. "I want to paint this box."

Father nods. "Good idea. You're a good painter."

"So are you," says Birdy.

"What color?" asks Father. "I seem to have lots of yellow."

"I love yellow!" says Birdy, excited. "The sun and night moons!"

I miss the quiet of Birdy's bedroom.

I turn the handle on the hall cupboard while everyone is talking and laughing.

Locked!

I try again.

Locked.

What is there to lock away in the cupboard? It's always held paper and supplies for school. And files for Mother and Father.

I look over at Ben. He always knows my looks. And what I'm asking. But Ben doesn't look my way.

Father picks up Tillie's litter box.

"You'll have to paint the box outside, Birdy. Let's go look for yellow."

He hands the litter box to Ben.

And they're out the door, Tillie slipping out with them.

I jiggle the cupboard handle again,

trying to turn it one way and the other.

Locked.

And then I hear Birdy scream outside.

I hurry out to the porch.

"No, Tillie!!" yells Birdy. "She'll leave claw marks!"

Tillie is climbing up Father's wood figure.

She hangs on to one spot, looking around.

Father goes over and gently rescues Tillie. He hands her to Ben.

"She sees a tree, you know," says Father.

Ben comes over, walking up the steps carrying Tillie.

"'Eyes and art,'" he comments to me, and we both laugh.

We put down a small bowl of cat snacks for Tillie.

"Okay, Nora," says Ben. "What's up? I saw your look."

"You always do," I say.

"Yep," says Ben. "The way of twins."

"It's the hall cupboard," I say. "It's locked!"

Ben smiles.

"You know something," I say.

Ben nods. He looks out the door at Birdy and Father, busy with paints. He moves to one side of the cupboard.

He points. Way behind the cupboard, almost hidden, is a key, hanging on a hook.

The key.

"You knew," I say.

Ben reaches and takes the key off the hook. He hands it to me.

I unlock the cupboard door.

"Be quick, Nora," he whispers.

Ben looks out the porch door, then comes over to look over my shoulder.

There are many papers inside. There's a stack of new notebooks for school. There are folders with our names on them. Nothing to lock away.

And then, I suddenly uncover a red

folder. I lift it out and read the name "Linnea" written there. The handwriting is Mother's.

Inside is a death notice for "Linnea Nilsson."

And a handwritten letter—Ben reads it over my shoulder as I read it out loud.

Dear friends Una and Geo,

    You are doing a wonderful thing for me and the beautiful Beatrix. You are making the end of my life full of joy, knowing you will love her as I do. The legal papers are enclosed.

    I have one last urgent important request that will make it hard for you—keeping a secret . . .

"Nora!! Close the door. Lock it!" says Ben quickly.

I hurry to put the file in order and close the door. I can feel my heart beating.

"I hear Father and Birdy calling us!" says Ben.

I lock the cupboard door. I lean way back behind the cupboard to hang the key on the wall hook.

"You all right?" asks Ben.

"Yes."

I look at Ben.

"I know what we have to do," I whisper.

Ben nods.

"The cemetery," Ben says quietly.

We go outside then, to see Birdy's litter box, painted with a bright sun on one side, night moons on the other.

And I smile again for Birdy.

And for her new "work of art."

11.

Tulips and Stone

Birdy stands up after a late lunch. Or is it early dinner?

Mother says we are "relaxed" about mealtimes.

"Goodbye. I'm going to play kick the can with Nico and other friends," says Birdy. "Tomorrow's Nico's birthday."

"Goodbye," echoes Father, standing, too. *"I'm* going to paint in falling light."

"Ben and I have an errand," I say.

"Now?" whispers Ben.

I nod.

Birdy and Nico are beginning their game as we walk down the street. They are laughing and kicking the can in the middle of the yard.

"Comforting," says Ben. "Watching them play is also calming. I call it the two *C*s."

"All that laughing and yelling. And running?" I ask.

"Calming," he says. "There is something

'everyday' about it."

"Everyday," I say, liking the sound of it.

Ben nods.

"Everyday," he repeats.

We pass the bakery. We pass the library. And we come to the cemetery.

"Ready?" Ben asks.

"Yep."

We open the gate and go in.

It is peaceful, the grass raked neatly between gravestones.

We know where the gravestone is my mother visits every week. Ben and I walk up to it.

Ben whispers the words on the stone.

"*Linnea Nilsson. Born: Stockholm, Sweden.*"

I point to the two etched words below—
Best Friend.

There is a vase of flowers there.

"Tulips and stone," I say. "Mother's flowers."

"Every week," says Ben in a soft voice.

I feel tears coming down my cheeks as we stand there.

It's quiet, the only noise the sound of a worker clearing weeds nearby.

I look at Ben and see tears in his eyes, too.

Ben lets me cry. I think of Miss Skylark, who always does the same.

Ben reaches over to brush fallen leaves from the stone top. Then we turn and walk away.

We open the gate and close it behind us.

We don't talk all the way home—past the library—past the bakery—stopping only to pat a friendly dog.

When we come to our street Ben looks over at me.

"We know things now," he says.

I nod. "Most things. Except . . ."

"Why the secret," Ben says. "Why keep the secret of Birdy."

I sigh.

"We have to unlock the cupboard again.
To finish reading Linnea's letter," I say.

"When we can," says Ben.

"I keep thinking of tulips and stone," I
say.

"Me, too," says Ben.

We walk silently again.

But when we walk up the steps—through
the back hallway and into the kitchen—all
things suddenly change.

12.

The Things We Know

Mother sits at the kitchen table, Father next to her.

"You're home!" I say. "How was the writing workshop?"

"Hi, Mom!" says Ben. "We hung your painting."

Mother and Father are both silent. Then Mother picks up a large envelope, holds it up, and drops it on the table.

I catch my breath. It's the secret DNA envelope addressed to Ben.

"Where's Birdy?" asks Ben quickly.

"She's at Nico's birthday party," says Father. He sighs. He sometimes sighs when he's waiting to hear what he hopes to hear. It's as if he fears that time will slip by.

"So you know," Ben says simply.

It's quiet.

"Tell them the beginning," I say to Ben.

He nods.

"Birdy put her spit in the envelope with

Mom's sample when no one was looking,"
Ben says.

He sits at the table.

"She sealed the envelope before it was
sent."

Father smiles a bit.

"Birdy?" he says softly. "Birdy began it
all?"

I sit down next to Ben.

"And when the return envelope came,
her paper fell out and we read it and kept
it," I say.

I take a breath.

"Birdy doesn't match either of you.
She's not Irish or Italian," I say quietly.

"And we thought it could be a mistake. So we decided to test it," Ben says.

There is silence still. I am suddenly angry. I stand up.

"And Birdy was right! She asked if you hadn't ever had a secret when she first got Tillie."

My voice rises.

"And you did! And that secret turned me into a keeper of secrets, too. Hiding secrets, finding a letter from Linnea in the cupboard that I couldn't finish reading!"

I feel tears coming.

Ben gets up and stands next to me, his arm around me.

"And today Nora and I went to the cemetery," he says, his voice calm.

"And when we talked to Miss Skylark at school . . ." I begin.

"You talked to Miss Skylark about this?" says Mother, shocked.

"We couldn't talk to you about it," says Ben calmly. "It is *your* secret."

Mother flinches as if she is hurt.

"Miss Skylark told us secrets are hard to keep. And she had only one question to ask us until the problem was solved."

I see Mother's eyes get wide.

Father reaches over to put his hand on her arm.

"What was her one question?" he asks in a soft voice.

"'Does it matter?' Does it matter where Birdy came from? We love her," Ben says.

"I hate secrets," I say. "Now we all have secrets. You started that."

I begin to leave the kitchen. I turn at the kitchen door.

"It goes on and on and on," I whisper in the quiet. "You won't love me for saying this."

I go down the hallway to my bedroom. I lock the door. I sit on my bed. I'm too tired to cry—too angry to cry.

Someone tries the doorknob to come

in. I don't move.

And then Father appears outside my window.

He opens it from the outside and climbs inside, a piece of lilac bush clinging to his shirt.

He sits on the bed next to me. He puts his arms around me.

"I'd love you and what you said no matter whose child you were," he says softly.

It's Father who has tears now.

And it's Father who will help us all understand the truth about Birdy.

13.

The Wood Child

Father and I sit on the bed for a while. He doesn't talk to fill a space, something I love about him. He has come to say what he wants to say and that's all.

"I'm practicing to be calm," I say softly.

He smiles.

"You're doing a swell job of it. And you were very strong in the kitchen just now."

"Where is Ben?" I ask.

"Still in the kitchen, skillfully convincing your mother of the power of the truth. Especially the truth for Birdy."

I smile and pick a piece of lilac off his shirt.

"Ben's a caretaker," I say. "Like you—climbing in my window."

"In some ways," says Father. "In other ways you and I are alike. I'm practicing to be calm, too."

He gets up and stands at the window.

"I see Birdy coming home," he says. "Do you want to go out the window with me? Or shall we unlock the door?"

I smile and unlock the door. The two of us go back to the kitchen.

We hold hands.

We are both calm.

Birdy comes into the kitchen, dressed up for Nico's birthday party.

"Milo's mother made a yarn ball toy for Tillie."

She tosses the ball in the air and Tillie streaks out from under a chair to catch and kill it.

"See that?" Birdy says.

She looks around at all of us then.

"What's wrong?"

"Well, Birdy," Father begins.

"Geo," Mother says quietly. "Let me begin."

Father nods.

"Birdy," Mother begins, "I have a secret to tell you."

"I knew you had a secret!" says Birdy, excited.

"I do remember," says Mother.

Birdy sits on Ben's lap, waiting. His arms go around her waist.

Mother smiles at her.

"The truth is . . . that I am not your first mother."

I feel goose bumps on my arms. The truth hangs in the air over us all.

Birdy stares at Mother. She doesn't move. She is silent.

Suddenly she smiles.

"You mean like Tillie? She had a mother cat. Now I'm her mother!"

Mother nods.

"Your first mother was my very best friend in the world. We went all through school together."

"Even Kinder Garden?" asks Birdy.

"Even kindergarten."

Then Birdy surprises us, mostly Mother.

"And did she die?" asks Birdy with a serious look.

I see tears in Mother's eyes.

"She did. She had you, a beautiful new baby she loved, but she was very sick with no family. And she wanted you to be in our family when she was gone!"

"And we loved you already," says Father.

Birdy looks at him.

"What about my true father?" she asks.

Mother shakes her head. "We don't know about him."

Father goes over and lifts Birdy off Ben's lap and into his arms.

"*I* am your true father," he says.

Birdy grins.

Father puts her down next to Mother.

"And—your first mother wanted us to wait to tell you about her until you were older. She wanted you to be happy in our family."

Mother takes Birdy's hand. "But we now know that was a mistake," she says.

"We wish she had known that being your parents is our joy," says Father.

"Joy," says Birdy softly. "Joy," she repeats as if she loves the word. And she says it again.

"I love that word, 'joy'!"

She looks at Mother, then Father.

"What was her name?"

Mother smiles.

"Linnea," says Father. "Her name was Linnea."

"That's a beautiful name!" says Birdy.

She looks up at Father.

"She was at your wedding in the field of blooms," says Birdy. "And when you find her picture I can put it up on my wall next to Mama's painting. The wall of the mothers!!"

I look at Ben. He smiles at me, but I know he is close to crying.

"Linnea means 'little flower' in Swedish," says Mother.

"Do you think Linnea would mind if I use her name for my middle name?" asks Birdy.

"Beatrix Linnea," says Mother.

"A fabulous name," says Father.

"She'd love that. And we'll visit her

grave where I visit every week," says Mother.

"Could I take her small little flowers for her Swedish name?" asks Birdy.

"Yes, you can. We'll go tomorrow."

"Can I take some of my favorite painted sea stones?"

Mother nods. "Linnea would like that. She loved to paint. And I'll tell you all about her—how we laughed—how we read books up in trees together—and how you made her happy."

Mother puts her arm around Birdy. "But I want you to know I was wrong to keep the secret," she says.

Birdy smiles.

"You should be celebrated!"

"I'm adopted! Like Nico!" says Birdy happily.

Father gets up and goes to the sun porch.

He brings back something wrapped in a blanket.

"I've been working on this for you."

He uncovers a sculpted wood child, the size of a baby. It is smooth and shining in the light.

He puts it on the table.

"This is you," he says.

"This is me?!" Birdy asks.

"You, Birdy," says Father.

Birdy runs her hands over the head of the child, the cheeks, the small hands with fingers curled into fists.

"It's yours to keep," says Father.

"In celebration of me!" Birdy says, looking at all of us. "I'm going to tell Nico we're both adopted!"

She takes the wood child into her arms. "And I'll show him *me!*"

And then Birdy is gone out the door— full of excitement—full of what she loves best—full of joy!

14.

A Poet's Truth

We sit quietly when Birdy leaves.

Finally Father smiles.

"Like the wind she goes," he says in the silence left behind.

Mother gets up and goes over to the kitchen counter and pours hot water from the kettle into her teacup.

Ben lifts his shoulders. I know he's about to say something. So far we have been silent.

"The words you said," he begins, watching Mother, "were very honest."

Mother sits down at the table. "So were *your* words. And Nora's," she says.

She looks thoughtful.

"A lie is dark and deep," she says.

Father looks at her and smiles a bit.

"I wrote that in my poetry class," she says.

"You know—it's amazing what the truth does for you. And *to* you."

"And *around* you," says Father.

"That, too," says Mother.

She takes two combs out of her hair

and goes over to the wastebasket and tosses them away.

"I think better without them," she says to us. "It's a celebration of *me*. I'm working tonight."

She smiles at us.

"That's the poet's truth," she says.

I see a look on Ben's face. He tilts his head toward the hallway.

"Where are we going?" I whisper as we leave the kitchen.

"Your bedroom. You have the best view."

In my room Ben goes right to my window.

"I knew it!" he says.

He begins to laugh. I haven't heard his laugh in a long time.

He points.

Birdy and Nico are playing kick the can in their birthday clothes.

I grin.

"Look under the lilac bush," says Ben.

Below the bush is Birdy's wood child, wrapped in its blanket.

"The celebration of Birdy," I say.

"It is," says Ben.

I lie down on my bed, leaning against a pillow.

"You're right," I say to Ben. "It *is* calming and comforting to hear them play outside."

"I know many things," says Ben, making me laugh.

"So, Father actually climbed in your window today?" Ben asks.

"Yes. He had lilac bush stuck to his shirt."

Ben smiles.

"He told me you were still in the kitchen talking to Mother about truth."

I peer over at Ben. "Actually, what did you tell Mother?"

He shrugs.

"'Truth is safe' is what I said."

We listen to the joyful voices outside my window—both of us comforted and calm.

"The two Cs," says Ben.

* * *

Later that night Ben and I look in on Birdy sleeping. The wood child is on a pillow beside her, wrapped in its blanket. Charles, her stuffed horse, is close. Tillie is curled in the quilt. The painted sea stones for Linnea are arranged in a circle of color on her bedside table.

Down the hall we see my mother's kitchen light.

"It's late," I say. "She told us she'd be working tonight."

"She wants to make the evening deadline for the morning newspaper," says Ben.

"And poets write at all hours," he adds.

He stands at my bedroom door.

I get into bed.

"Open or shut?" Ben asks.

"Open, please," I say. "I want to listen to the clicking of Mother's keyboard."

He smiles at me.

"Our ritual," he says. "I always go to bed later than you do."

For a while I watch the stars out my window.

Then I turn over.

And I listen to the clicking of a poet writing in the night—

until I sleep.

15.

Linked

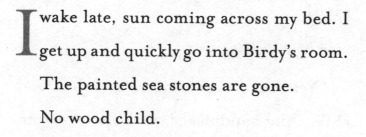

I wake late, sun coming across my bed. I get up and quickly go into Birdy's room.

The painted sea stones are gone.

No wood child.

I pick up Charles the horse and sit on Birdy's scrambled bed, hold him in my arms.

And I know.

Birdy and Mother have gone to the cemetery.

To Linnea's grave.

I sit there for a long time.

Ben and Father are sitting at the kitchen table. Father is drawing in a large sketchbook with a pen. He looks up and smiles at me.

"They're gone?" I ask.

"Yes. Carrying sea stones and the wood child. And handpicked small flowers from the garden."

Ben is eating cereal with raspberries. He points to Charles, still in my arms.

I put Charles in his lap as he eats.

He moves the open newspaper on the table.

"Mom made her deadline," he says quietly.

"I heard the night clicking," I say.

Father gets up and pours a glass of juice for me.

"Thanks."

He taps my shoulder and goes back to his sketchbook. I sit down and read the column.

Una's View
The Three of Me
The three of me are—
The Columnist.

The Mother.

The Poet.

You know me as a columnist.

I invite responses. And you respond.

The Columnist of me.

An important part of me is my family.

My children taught me this.

The Mother of me.

I know a mother who kept a big secret

for a long time. She thought it was best.

But her children taught her a secret can

become a lie. They taught her the truth is

safe. And truth can be forgiving.

I know this.

I am that mother.

The third part of me I call "The Poet of

me."

I tell my truth in a new personal way.

A lie is deep and dark,
tangled in my words—
    my head—
    my heart!
    until truth shines it away—
    Leaving joy!

—Una Rossi

I rub tears away with the back of my hand. Father hands me his folded handkerchief. He flips a page over in his sketchbook.

Ben reaches over to me—his hand out.

I reach out too. We link fingers.

"Don't move," Father says to us suddenly.

Ben and I stay linked. Father sketches, the only sound his pen on paper.

"No more secret," says Ben quietly, our fingers still linked.

"And Birdy celebrating," I say.

"I'm thinking Miss Skylark will be happy to hear it."

Father flips his page for another sketch.

Ben grins at me.

"And *I'm* thinking Birdy will be happy telling Miss Skylark."

Even Father laughs at this as he sketches.

It is oddly comfortable and peaceful for

me and Ben to stay linked.

"Okay!" Father says. "You can let go."

Ben laughs.

"I'd almost forgotten," he says.

"I'm not surprised," says Father. "You two were born with linked fingers."

"Really?!" says Ben.

Father nods.

He turns his sketchbook around for us to see.

"Then," he says. "A sketch remembered."

It's a sketch of tiny baby fingers, linked.

He flips the paper again.

"And now," he says. "A sketch of today.

"I saw it when you were born—when you were little —and now."

Father looks at his sketches.

"Yep," he says, pleased with them. "Linked."

16.

"This Is Great!"

"I'm back!" calls Birdy. She carries the wood child and a heavy tote bag.

Mother comes behind, her hair wind-blown.

Birdy sits down at the table.

"I put little white flowers on Linnea's grave, and I made a design with my sea stones. The caretaker likes them and says he'll look over them and play with them."

She sets the wood child on the table.

"And!" she adds. "He called me 'sweetish.'"

Mother smiles.

"'Swedish,' that is," she says quietly.

Father gets up and puts his arms around Birdy.

"I think you're 'sweetish,'" he says.

"What's in your tote bag?"

Birdy grins. "Library books!"

She pulls them out of her bag, one after another, counting them, "one, two, three, four," until we stop her.

"They only let me take out twelve books," she complains.

"But *this* is the best of all!" says Birdy. "Mama bought me this!" She pulls out a large notebook. "I love books. Now I can write my own words!"

She looks at all of us.

"Why not?!" she says, her hands held out in the "why not" look.

"Why not," says Father.

"And you can paint the illustrations for my writing," Birdy tells Father.

"Yep. In my spare time," he says, making Mother burst out laughing.

"This is great," says Birdy.

She picks up her bag of books, her notebook, and the wood child. Ben puts Charles the horse in her arms, too.

Tillie runs into the kitchen, happy to see Birdy.

"All this!" says Birdy, stopping at the kitchen door, looking back at us. "This is *great!*"

And Birdy hurries down the hall to her room.

It's a quiet afternoon.

Father is in his studio. Ben and Birdy are in their rooms.

I sit on my bed and think about Mother and her words. I go looking for her.

"You're not at your desk," I say, surprised.

I look at her caller ID.

"You have three calls from the newspaper. No messages left."

Mother nods. She's cooking, pots of pasta and sauce on the stove, a large salad on the counter.

She turns, leaning against the sink. "I turned off my computer. Want the truth? I'm nervous about this morning's column."

I reach over and take her hand.

"Want *my* truth?" I say. "I love what you wrote. Your readers will, too."

Mother puts her arms around me.

"Your words had everything to do with it," she says.

She pushes her hair out of her eyes and takes a large red ribbon out of her pocket.

"A favor, Nora? Tie my hair back in this ribbon? It will make cooking easier."

She grins at my look.

"Birdy bought it for me today," she says. "With her own allowance money."

I tie her hair back in a red bow. I feel like a mother caring for a child.

"What's happening here?" asks Ben, coming into the kitchen. He stares at Mother.

"Oh wow! Red!" he says, making me and Mother laugh.

"Where's Birdy?" asks Mother.

"In her room, becoming a writer," says Ben.

The phone rings.

Mother sighs. She wipes her hands and goes over to her desk.

"Hello?" She closes her eyes, listening. Then she quickly sits up.

"What? Are you serious?!"

She listens more.

"I'll turn on my computer. I promise."

She hangs up. She turns on her computer and prints a paper and reads it.

Father comes into the kitchen.

Mother hands him the paper. She looks shocked.

"The newspaper got hundreds of replies to my column," she says. "This was their most astonishing and different response." Father reads it.

"For Una Rossi:

Where have you been 'The Poet of me?!'

We love the poet—the voice finds us and

stays and becomes us. Just as your poetry

is you. More please!

—Lily, Marcus, Heidi, Emma, William,

Justin, Rudy, Neal, and eighty others. We

are parents, teachers, readers, and writers

who support you!"

"The newspaper wants me to write poems whenever I want—and call that part of my work 'The Poet of Me.'"

"Beautiful sense," says Ben, as I knew he would—in the way of twins.

Father smiles at Mother.

"What, Geo?" she asks.

"I smile at the good news for you," he says. "I smile for the poet of you. *And* I smile at the big red ribbon," says Father.

He puts his arms around Mother.

"As Birdy would say, 'This is great!'" he says.

17.

"My Joy"

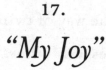

We eat dinner, Mother's hair loose now. Her red ribbon is rolled up neatly on the spice rack, between garlic powder and ginger.

Birdy sits on her new notebook.

After dinner Father leans over and points to it.

"Your writing?" he asks.

Birdy nods.

"I only have a beginning and middle. Not the right ending yet," she says. "And I don't have a name for what I wrote."

This makes Father smile. "Sometimes I begin a work and I don't know the end."

"With writing, too," adds Mother.

"I remember the bird that flew in and out of your painting," says Birdy. "You were surprised."

"And remember Dad's dead tree," says Ben.

"This isn't those things at all," says Birdy. "You'll see."

Birdy unearths the notebook from

under her. She opens it and reads to us.

My Joy
Joy is every day,
　　left to me by my first mother.
Joy is laughter
　　and secrets kept—
　　　　finding my toad in the dark.
Joy is the wood child
　　next to me at night
　　　　so I sleep with the child I was.
Joy is the painting of my mother
　　watching over me when I sleep.

Birdy closes her notebook. She leans back in her chair. She opens her hands as if to say *What do you think?*

"That's very, very good," says Ben, looking surprised.

"Beautiful," says Mother.

Birdy looks at me.

"I have a name for what you wrote," I
say.

She grins.

"You have written a poem, Birdy," I tell
her.

"Yes," says Mother.

Birdy sighs.

"I thought so," she says.

"Remember what Miss Skylark told you?
She said: 'You'll soon be a writer,'" I say.

Father leans over and takes a wrapped
package out from under his chair.

"I think Una and I have the ending to your poem," he says.

"What?" asks Birdy.

Father hands her the package.

Birdy unwraps it. She looks at a photograph of a smiling woman. Her smile is bright like Birdy's smile.

Birdy stares at it. Then smiles.

Birdy knows.

"Linnea," she whispers.

She looks at us. She smiles.

"Linnea!"

It's dusk. We're all in Birdy's room.

Mother leans against a pillow, Charles the horse on her lap. Ben and I crowd next to her, Ben holding the wood child.

I point to more sea stones on the bedside table, waiting for paint.

"She has a basket full under the bed," Ben whispers to me.

Tillie comes into the room with her *blurp!* sound of surprise to see us all there. She jumps up on the bed and sits next to Mother.

Birdy stands at the window, looking for Nico.

"Kick the can later?" Mother asks her.

"Yes!" says Birdy. "It's my everyday life!"

I smile at Ben. "Everyday life" is an expression of his.

"'Everyday life' sounds like 'beautiful

sense,'" says Father.

He holds up the framed photograph of Linnea. He points to a place next to his painting of Mother.

"Yes," says Birdy. She watches him hang the picture.

"There it is," he says to Birdy.

Birdy looks at the two pictures next to each other.

"My two mothers watching over me when I sleep," recites Birdy in her quiet voice.

She smiles.

"The perfect ending to my poem."

She looks at all of us.

"'My Joy,'" she says.

There are no more words to say.

I look at Ben, close to me on the bed.

He smiles and nods at me as if he hears my thought. And, in the way of twins, I know that Ben and I are thinking the very same thing—

The perfect ending to the story of Birdy.

Start reading Patricia MacLachlan's
MY LIFE BEGINS!

1.

"The Trips"

I am nine years old when my life begins.
Before then, I was the only child. The
son of Maeve and Daniel Black.

My baby picture hangs on the large
living room wall all by itself. My name,
"Jacob," is printed in the margin below my
face.

"I look lonely," I say.

"I think 'serious' is the word, Jacob," says my father. "Or 'solemn.'"

I don't like either word.

"We need more happy pictures," I say.

"My friend Bella's dog has a litter of puppies. Maybe we can get puppies."

"Soon we'll have babies," says Mother. "Remember?"

"Not puppies," I say.

"Not now," says Father. "Soon we'll have happy faces."

"Very soon," says Mother, looking tired and big.

"But the babies will be *yours*," I say. "Maybe *one puppy*?"

No one answers me.

Then on a late winter day it happens.

The "Trips" are born. That's my name for the triplets who are born—Charlotte, Katherine, and Elizabeth.

They will soon become—

"Char,"

"Kath,"

"Liz."

It's a little like a litter of puppies.

I write in my notebook:

"A Litter of Trips"

The Trips are here.

They're not pretty.

They look like birds without feathers.

Puppies are cuter.

—Jacob

I am only nine, remember. But I can tell right away that it will be my job to study and train the Trips. My mother and father are too tired for that.

Their first months, days and nights, are full of sleep and waking to feed the Trips with sterilized bottles of formula and mother's milk. And constant diaper changing—the diapers are the size of party napkins.

"Puppies would be easier," I say to Father.

"True," he says, yawning.

The kitchen is full of bottles. Sometimes I have to search for apples, oranges, bread, or milk for my cereal.

Father puts a small refrigerator for me in the pantry. I can find my milk, juice, snacks, and ice cream. The pantry is mine. I don't mind. It's out of the way.

More than once I find Father in there, just leaning against the counter in the quiet.

I lean against the counter, too.

"I'd like a puppy," I say.

"Yes," says Father.

"Yes, I can *have* one?"

"Yes, I know you want one," he says wearily.

The Trips are identical, so Mother dresses them in separate colors to tell them apart:

blue for Char,

red for Kath,

yellow for Liz.

They wear tiny bracelets with the same colors and their names. That seems strangely sad to me. After all, they've been curled up together inside my mother for months.

When my friends Allie and Thomas come to my house they are startled.

"What are those, Jacob?" Thomas asks, pointing to the beds. Thomas always asks questions when he knows the answers. He

once explained to me that it gives him time
to think.

"My litter of puppies," I say.

Thomas ignores my joke.

"Three," Thomas says, staring at them.

"Triplets," I say.

"They are all the same," says Allie.

She means "identical."

"They *look* the same," I say. "Mother says
they'll change."